THE BELMONT

BARR / DALTON

Published by Barr26 Publishing, LLC | www.Barr26Publishing.com

Rick Barr | www.Barr26.com/narrator

Michele Pollock Dalton | www.MichelePollockDalton.com

The Belmont

Miss May

Jazz musician, Bobby Troup, had immortalized the dusty old highway years earlier with his song, "Get Your Kicks on Route 66." But Lucas Barnes couldn't find a single thing "kicking" in the little town midway between Springfield, Illinois and St. Louis, Missouri. Instead, derelict buildings stood as sad sentinels along the cracked stretch of roadway – a dismal monument to a bygone era.

Grimly, Lucas pulled into the gravel parking lot at his destination, then heaved out a feral growl and a string of profanities directed at his absent, money-grubbing cousin. "Damn you, Richie!" he scowled as he surveyed the "opportunity of a lifetime."

Grabbing his cell phone from the backpack wedged between his hip and the pile of belongings on the front seat, Luc punched the "call" button and waited for his miscreant, scum-sucking, mercenary cousin to answer. "What in the hell?" he shouted down the line when the call connected.

Rich Levy rolled his eyes in exasperation and waited for the onslaught on the other end to die down before calmly replying. "I told you. The Belmont is an investment, Luc. That's a quarter of a million-dollar property you got there!"

"It's a block full of dilapidated buildings," Lucas rejoined, cursing himself as every kind of fool.

"What exactly did you expect for twenty-five grand? The Ritz-Carlton? Get a grip!" Rich contemptuously muttered. After shrugging the tension from his shoulders and smoothing a hand over his silk tie, Rich cajoled, "The Belmont is on the National Register – it's a landmark of American history.

And, you got it for a steal of a deal!"

Profanity dripped from his lips like venom as Lucas ran wary eyes over the hulking shells of what was once a thriving enterprise. A compound of four commercial buildings and two houses dotted the otherwise barren lot. Even plant life had abandoned the miserable piece of real estate.

Ignoring the other man's frustrated mumblings, Rich expounded, "My father's aunt May played piano in the café there for thirty years, and she always had plenty of tall tales to tell of the musicians that graced the small stage." Richie paused and waited for a comment. When none was forthcoming, he grumbled, "You wanted a songwriting retreat, Lucas. And, you got it. Now stop bugging me and get on with it!"

Huffing out a disgruntled breath, Lucas disconnected the call and tossed his cell phone onto the dash of his beat-up 1954 Chevy Pickup.

The late afternoon sunshine was dipping steadily toward the horizon, and Luc needed to get his borrowed camper set up before he lost the last of the light. With resigned acceptance, he parked near one of the garage bays of the defunct service station. After a quick peek through the grime-covered windows, Lucas chose a likely candidate and hoisted the roll-up door.

Disgust warped Luc's features as he peered into the gloomy cavern filled with miscellaneous junk. "Good grief!" he groused when the odor of old oil and the dust of decades nearly choked him. Since overnight temperatures would likely drop toward freezing, Lucas decided the protection of the smelly old building was preferable to his nards going numb; but he certainly wasn't pleased by the prospect of sheltering in the rundown structure.

Half an hour later, the irritable man stomped around in search of a place to plug in the extension that powered everything in his camper. Luc jostled a leaning tower of bald-faced tires out of the way as he looked for an outlet. When he'd signed the closing papers on the property a week earlier, the real estate agent assured him the utilities would be connected before his arrival. Yeah, right!

"Damn it!" he growled at the hulking body of a rusted-out Plymouth Barracuda. With filthy hands, he shoved the sweaty hair back from his forehead before he dropped them to his hips in tight fists. At the end of his proverbial rope, Lucas marched out to his truck and yanked the big emergency flashlight from the glove box.

There was a bite in the breeze, and sweeping air currents chased the storm of falling leaves into mini twisters that danced across the broken pavement around the antiquated gas pumps near the front of the station.

Buffeted by the wind, Lucas tugged the front of his flannel shirt closed and aimed the glow of the flashlight at the other low-slung structures on his property. The two buildings that formed the L-shaped motel might be questionable in terms of habitation, but Luc figured it was worth finding out if they had power.

Tentatively, he made his way across the open space between the service station and the original café – once again wondering about the absence of grass or trees.

On his way past the larger of the two houses on the property, he stopped and illuminated the peeling paint on the structure before he realized that there wasn't a single indication of life in a several block radius. Lucas hadn't paid much attention to the abandoned buildings across the street earlier, but the absence of light and sound made him squirrely. In fact, the whole scene reminded him of something out of a post-apocalyptic thriller. And after the incessant noise and energy of Chicago, the silence was deafening. Unnerving . . . and creepy.

The crunch of gravel under his feet was inordinately loud when Luc traveled over the area reserved for parking in front of the old restaurant, but once he had a clear view of the ramshackle eatery, his mood skyrocketed. An intermittent glow beckoned him up the lopsided concrete steps, and Lucas shone his light through the front window.

Startled by a gaunt, disheveled image in the glass, Luc jumped in surprise and then groaned at his own gullibility. With a bemused chuckle, Lucas chided himself for getting the bejesus scared out of him by his own shadow. Chagrined, he scrubbed at the grime on his face with the back of his sleeve. There wasn't much improvement in his reflection when Luc checked the plate glass a second time, but at least the apparition wore a smile this time around.

Unable to distinguish the source of the brightness, Lucas dropped the beam of his flashlight and pressed his face against the glass for a better look.

When the door moved in response to the press of his body, Luc gave it an annoyed shove and stared in dazed disbelief as it swung open.

"What do I need with twenty different keys if they didn't bother to lock things up?" he grumbled to the chilly night air as he brought his flashlight to bear. Swinging the beam from side to side, Luc gave a frustrated groan when he discovered more teetering piles of junk, and the beleaguered man scowled.

Traipsing past an upended group of dust encrusted mattresses, Lucas found a small opening near the serving counter and used the vantage point to scope out the layout of the seating area. There was a low hum of static in the air, and Luc was determined to find the power source!

Moving cautiously, Luc worked his way around the relics of years long past – at least until he inadvertently bumped into a stack of chrome dining chairs. The resultant crash and domino effect of falling odds and ends was a deafening cacophony until the last of the mattresses fell with a hollow "ooof."

Waving away the storm clouds of dust, Lucas hacked and coughed until his chest ached. "For the love of god!" he bellowed when he could breathe again. How the hell was he supposed to get back through the scattered shambles?

Mere seconds later, Luc shouted, "You've got to be kidding me!" as the beam of his flashlight faded and then went dark. Tipping his head back, Lucas stared into the inky darkness above him and wondered exactly what he'd done to exasperate the Almighty. Cause there certainly couldn't be any other explanation for the day he was having!

The skittering and squeaking of the café's four-legged residents gave Lucas the heebie-jeebies, and he took a small step back. Thankful when the heel of his well-worn boot hit the step to the stage, Lucas took the offered route of escape – just in time to avoid the miniature hoard of fleeing rodents.

When the disgruntled populace was quiet once again, Luc returned his attention to the aggravating errand. Then he noticed that the white noise had become more pronounced. It shifted, resolved, and became a soft, tinny version of a familiar tune.

"Tell me, dear, are you lonesome tonight?" Presley lowly crooned into the murky darkness.

"Well, crap on a cracker!" Lucas joyfully mused. There was power - a situation which definitely called for a celebration, he decided with a grin.

"Now the stage is bare, and I'm standing there with emptiness all around," the King continued – his voice resonating through the room, all traces of static gone.

Lucas listened in appreciation of the classic, but as the music faded, he was puzzled by the distinct "scratch, scratch" – a long-forgotten sound that followed a song when the phonograph needle came to the end of a vinyl record.

"Hello?" Lucas called, aggravated and a bit worried at the thought of a vagrant holed up somewhere nearby. "Who's there?" he tried again.

The swinging door between the seating area and the kitchen moved slightly, and a shadow separated itself from the blackness.

"I don't mean any harm," a soft voice explained.

Shocked into silence, Lucas squinted his eyes and tried to make out the shape of his unexpected guest, but the almost undiscernible "whoosh" of the door swinging closed convinced Luc that his visitor had retreated. "You can't stay here!" he hotly advised.

A quiet, lilting bit of laughter was the response from the kitchen, but Luc forgot his pique with the stranger when a dim glow shimmered and then brightened across the room. The subtle illumination drew Lucas' attention. As he tripped and stumbled his way across the chaotic space, Luc was able to make out the domed shape of an old-fashioned, tabletop jukebox.

As one of many, the well-preserved antique was a pleasant surprise. Crowded into the serving window with its mates, the jukebox drew Luc's curiosity. He ran a finger over the row of selection buttons at the bottom of the machine. Then Lucas turned the chrome wheel and watched the little tabs containing the song names rotate. "Someone must have been an Elvis fan," he absently commented as he read off the titles.

"Yes," replied the wistful voice from the kitchen.

Startled by the reminder of the trespasser, Luc grumbled, "You can't stay here."

"I heard you the first time," the young woman saucily rejoined.

Distracted by the conversation, it took Lucas a moment to discover the fading glow of the jukebox. "Hey!" he protested. "Turn that back on! I need to see where it's plugged in!" In the silence, Luc waited for a reply. But the only response was the feedback of the phonograph needle as it settled into the groove. Then the distinctive sound of an acoustic guitar filled the air, followed by the backup singers, and Elvis' questioning, "Are you lonesome tonight . . ."

"Come on. Not this again," Lucas groused before he fumbled his way along the counter to the swinging door. He pushed against the chrome hand plate and grunted. The darn thing wouldn't budge! "Listen, lady! Don't make me call the cops."

The wicked screech of the needle being yanked across the record made Luc cringe, and he imagined there was a nasty scratch left in the vinyl. "Lady?" Luc called.

Another hard shove propelled him through the portal, and Lucas skidded to a stop when he crashed into the corner of a table. Rubbing at the pain behind his zipper, Luc bent and propped his hands on his knees. "Damn it!" he huffed as he cupped his sore balls. In vexation, Lucas cursed again before he kicked at the offending piece of furniture with his steel-toed boots. "Stupid piece of junk! I'm having a bonfire tomorrow, and you're going to be the first thing I toss in!" he hissed at the sturdy butcher block prep table.

Haley Mitchell bit back a grin as she listened to the man's diatribe. When the call had come in, she'd turned her squad toward The Belmont with the usual bit of frustration. The abandoned buildings were a prime site for teenage mischief, especially as Halloween approached. But Officer Mitchell was surprised to find a grown man lumbering about inside the clandestine hangout. "Sir. I'll need you to join me outside," she stated with authority before turning her flashlight on the suspect.

Blinded, Lucas shot a protective hand toward his face.

Gesturing the man forward with the beam of light, Haley placed the other hand on her firearm and anxiously waited for the vagrant's compliance. Backing away from the rear entrance of the café as the man approached, Haley demanded, "Hands up against the wall, please."

"It's my place," Lucas protested while the officer patted him down and questioned his presence. "If you want a trespasser, look for the woman who's been camping out here."

"Woman?" Officer Mitchell questioned dubiously.

"Yeah! I didn't get a look at her in the dark, but she sounded young," Lucas explained as he tried to find a comfortable stance. Fighting the unmitigated urge to place a protective hand over his aching private parts, Lucas attempted to keep his voice even. "Just look for a fugitive with a record player and a penchant for Presley."

Haley snorted, then chuckled in disbelief. "Alright, mister. Joke's on me," the woman admitted. "So, who hired you? Captain Drake? Lieutenant Roberts?"

Quirking an eyebrow, Lucas slowly turned his head and sent a questioning glance at the policewoman.

"Seriously. Who put you up to this?" she inquired.

Perplexed, Luc cocked his head and wondered what weird Twilight Zone episode he'd wandered into.

"Okay, Mr. Barnes," Haley relented. "We'll forget about this, but tell your buddies I'm not going to fall for another one of their Halloween pranks. Got it?" she directed. "Oh, and stay out of these old buildings. I don't want anyone getting hurt on my watch."

"Ah, ma'am. I don't mean any disrespect . . . but what in the hell are you talking about?" Luc scowled. His attitude might land him in the county lock-up, but at the moment, Lucas was beyond caring.

Delighted to match wits with the stranger, Haley decided to play along. "You've seen Miss May, huh?" she lightly questioned, already anticipating the answer.

"Didn't get her name," Lucas grunted. "Can I turn around now? It's weird having a conversation with this wall."

The squawk of her car radio drew Haley's attention for a minute, but then she contemplated the disheveled man. "You are free to go, Mr. Barnes. I need to get back to my patrol."

"Hey! Wait just a minute. Are you going to look for the real trespasser or not?" Lucas growled as he faced off with the lady officer. "I don't want to press charges, but like you said – it's not safe for people to be wandering around here. You find that girl and tell her that."

"Tell Drake or Roberts . . . whoever put you up to this . . . that I appreciated their efforts. But, the joke is over."

Cutting the woman off, Lucas snapped, "What joke? There was a squatter in one of my buildings. And, who knows how long she's been there!"

Huffing out an exasperated sigh over the actor's insistence, Haley moved toward her vehicle as she glibly replied, "Seventy years, give or take."

"Say what?" Lucas demanded, following along behind the officer.

Officer Mitchell rolled her eyes and humored the prankster. "Miss May's got a thing for the King of Rock n'Roll, and if you run into her again, give her a chocolate milkshake. Supposedly, she'll happily drift off to the corner booth and moon over her lost lover."

Confused, Lucas watched the zany policewoman settle into her squad car. "I'm not running a shelter for Elvis groupies!"

Hayley chuckled. "If you've met May Levy, then I guess you are . . . running a shelter for Elvis groupies, I mean," she teased. "According to local folklore, Miss May doesn't introduce herself to just anyone. You must be something special."

Befuddled by the mocking woman, Lucas backed away from the vehicle as it began to move.

Grinning, Haley waved at the disgruntled fellow. "Welcome to Litchfield, Mr. Barnes. I hope you enjoy your stay at The Belmont."

Piffles

The rich tones of the hand-crafted guitar in his hands soothed Lucas Barnes' ruffled nerves. After a nearly sleepless night huddled in the frigid camper, the warmth of the early afternoon sunshine thawed the stiffness that had lingered all morning.

As Luc fiddled with a new tune, he twanged out, "Now, I'm livin' on the honky-tonk side of town . . . that's where you go when life gets you down."

He punched through the lyrics with a heavy country sound and muddled over the next musical phrase. With a bit of inspiration from his surroundings, Lucas continued, "It's a one-way ticket to the wrong side of the tracks. When you hit the honky time . . . there ain't no goin' back!"

Satisfied with the impromptu chorus, Luc chuckled at his new theme song and decided it needed at least one verse.

"Run down buildings . . . late model cars,
Slum lords, their captives . . . and backstreet bars.
I'm sorry to say . . . I've finally found,
The dead-end road to the honky-tonk side of town."

A wry grin suggested that Lucas had emerged from his funk as he played through his newest effort a second time. Then a third.

When the utility truck from the electric cooperative pulled up street side, Lucas gently laid his "pride and joy" in its case and tucked the Lowden in with more care than a mother with her newborn.

"Boy, am I glad to see you," he greeted when the lineman approached.

"If you can't figure out what's going on with the power in this place, I'm going to freeze to death."

"We'll get some temporary lines up for you, sir. But you'll want an electrician to check things before we tie-in to the buildings."

"Tie-in?" Lucas irritably questioned. Following the lineman's gesture, Luc glanced at the creosote covered pole on the corner and scrunched up his face. "Hold up. I'm not following you," he finally mumbled as the other man rambled along. "First off, if I need an electrician, I'm hoping you can make a recommendation. And, second? Why do I need temporary lines? What's something like that cost?" Lucas questioned in trepidation. His limited budget couldn't take too many surprises if he hoped to host his first songwriting retreat come spring.

Waving widely between the poles, the employee explained, "That wind storm we had 'bout five years ago brought down most of the lines on this side of town. And, since there weren't any active customers over this way, the cooperative decided against re-stringing this area. Eventually, they plan on running underground lines, but for now, we'll get something up to get you in service."

Luc was beginning to feel like a parrot. "In service?" he repeated.

"Yup. It'll take me most of the day," the lineman acknowledged. "Gotta bring new lines about three blocks." Riffling through his pockets, the fellow found the crumpled, yellowed business card he carried. "Give this guy a call. He's the electrician most folks around here use. And, if you tell him it's for The Belmont, Hank'll likely make it a priority. It was his people who started this place back in the '20s."

* * * * *

Luc's mind returned to the previous night's "adventure" as he worked. Without electrical service, how had the jukebox lit up? And if it was nothing more than a prank, why would anyone go to such elaborate lengths to taunt the new guy in town? None of it made any sense!

Stretched to his full height at the top of a rickety ladder, Lucas held his breath and hurriedly twisted the last fluorescent tube into the suspended fixture. A mixture of relief and revulsion flooded him when the interior of the old garage was revealed in all of its grubby glory.

His balance faltered when an angry buzzing in the air resolved into another Elvis classic. "You look like an angel," the King began - much to Luc's annoyance.

"Enough with the tricks!" he kvetched. "I don't have times for your games."

"This place is a mess," a pony-tailed blonde observed, her pink poodle skirt swishing as she moved into Luc's line of sight.

Moving down the ladder, Lucas mumbled at the girl through the rungs, "You look like a reject from the set of 'Grease.'"

A haughty eyebrow went up, and the young woman indignantly crossed her arms over her chest. "If you would clean this place up, then I wouldn't have an oil stain on my favorite skirt," she complained.

Rolling his eyes, Luc ignored the sassy hooligan and looked around for the origin of the sound. "Listen, kid, I've got more than enough to do without being your primary source of entertainment," he admonished. "Go bother someone else!"

Disbelief blossomed on Luc's face when the enraged girl charged the ladder and hit him full force. A frigid blast surged through his bloodstream on impact, and Lucas convulsed in shock as his limbs went lax. Panic choked him, and Luc mentally braced for impact with the hard concrete below. But his numb body held its form, and Lucas peered out at the hazy world through the back of his eyeballs. The perception of distance . . . it was strange. Holy hell! He could see the reverse side of his orbital ridge!

Luc had heard of getting the stuffing knocked out of you, but his current situation? It was the exact reverse. He felt a bit like an astronaut . . . trapped inside his suit . . . staring out at the great beyond through the lensed helmet. Incredulous, Lucas tried to yell at the troublemaker - only to find the sound echoed inside his head. He pounded at the back of what was surely his own ribcage and demanded release - only to feel a low chuckle rumble through the chest cavity.

Locked inside of his own body, Luc's frenzied thoughts scattered when agony detonated and scorched his nervous system. Flailing, he resumed the use of his mortal form – just in time to realize that he was falling. The crack of the concrete against his tailbone truncated the hoarse yell of surprise lodged in Lucas' throat and turned it into convulsive retching.

"Heaven help me, I didn't see the devil in your eyes," Elvis commiserated as Luc heaved up his dinner.

The bitter smell of bile and the rancid taste in his mouth assured Lucas he was once again in full possession of his faculties – as if the misery in his back wasn't indication enough. The metal rods that stabilized fused vertebrae screamed without mercy as Luc shifted enough to spit out the remaining chunks of vomit that clogged his throat.

"Oh!" a soft voice cried. "Are you okay?"

"Stay . . . away . . . from me," Lucas gasped, still in the throes of torment.

"Piffles!" May screeched. "You leave this poor man alone!"

* * * * *

When his eyes lurched open, Lucas warily eyed the young woman who moved about the tiny confines of his pop-up camper. "Go away," he groaned.

Unfazed, May sat down at the small dinette and sent mournful looks at the interloper. "Well, now you've done it," she quietly observed. The man's pain-filled eyes urged her to be quiet, but May was obligated to warn the stranger. "You shouldn't be messing around in the service station. This is Piffles' territory."

Luc ignored the comment and hoarsely rejoined, "As soon as I can move, I'm calling the police."

May twisted her hands together and looked at her lap. "Um, you really don't want to mess with Primrose Piffles. He's not a, um, . . . not a nice soul, I guess you'd say." Looking up through her lashes, May gave an awkward shrug of her shoulders, and then she nervously smoothed the fabric of the fire-engine red pencil skirt she was wearing.

Unable to help himself, Lucas scoffed, "Primrose?"

Giggling, May met the upset fellow's gaze. With a nod of her head, she tittered before she sobered and covered her mouth. "He won't like it if he thinks we are laughing at him," May confided. "That name caused him no end of trouble when we were younger."

"I don't care. Just get out of my sight and off my property."

With a deep sigh, May sent a piercing glance at the angry mortal. "I live here," she explained. "I'm as much a part of The Belmont as the buildings."

"Out!" Lucas shouted with the last of his energy. He squinted in astonishment and looked around. The irritating girl was gone - there and gone in the blink of an eye! Miserable and aggravated, Luc considered his condition and concluded that he must be concussed. There was no other explanation for the strange interaction or the episode on the ladder. And, come to think of it . . . how had he ended up in the camper?

Exhausted, Lucas reached for the pain reliever and the glass of water next to his bed. As he was drifting off, it occurred to him to question the presence of the narcotic. But sleep took over, and another piece of the puzzling situation was left unanswered.

* * * * *

Drenched in sweat, Luc shoved the covers away from his chest and gingerly rolled to his aching back. His scream pierced the air when he came face to face with a ghoulish apparition hovering directly above him. Bug-eyed, he clawed at the pressure around his Adam's apple as the specter descended. Locked in frantic combat with the fearsome poltergeist, Lucas struggled to break free – his mind fogged by disbelief and terror.

"Primrose Piffles pees his pants, pees his pants, pees his pants," a merry voice singsonged from near Luc's left ear.

Incensed, the maniacal presence transferred his attention to his supernatural counterpart, and Piffles roared obscenities at the irreverent young woman who mocked him. Distracted by the girl's taunting, his malevolent energy shifted, and his shape drifted into the representation of his previously mortal body.

Fearful and furious at the same time, Luc heaved his body upward and dislodged the balding, rotund, middle-aged spook.

May broke off her chanting long enough to encourage Lucas to pick-up the refrain. And, once his raspy voice joined hers, May changed her provoking tune to: "Poopy Piffles sniffles."

"What in the hell was that?" Lucas demanded when the enraged spirit burst into fiery particles and vanished. The scent of brimstone hung heavy in the air and Luc waved it away with a trembling hand.

"That was Primrose Piffles," May advised in a huff. "I told you not to mess with him, but you wouldn't listen."

"MESS. WITH. HIM?" Luc bellowed. "I was sleeping!"

"Pffft! You were sleeping in his garage. And, you were messing around with his junk today. I saw that pile of tires you left out by the road," she corrected like a proper schoolmarm.

Rolling into an awkward sitting position, Lucas scrubbed at his face and stared at the irritating girl. Despite the absence of illumination, he could still see her very clearly. "So, what are you exactly? And why were we making fun of that . . . that thing?"

May settled primly into her place at the dinette and surveyed the perturbed fellow. The ebony hair and blue eyes were a keen reminder of another man . . . the one who'd stolen her heart. Suddenly shy, May extended her hand. "I'm May. May Levy," she softly greeted. "And, I guess I am . . . a memory. A memory woven into the fabric of this place."

"You're a ghost," Lucas asserted with a disgruntled air.

Chagrined, the girl scrunched her face up and disagreed. "I don't wear bedsheets and fly through walls! I . . . well, I just don't have the same physical limitations you do," she proclaimed, satisfied with the answer.

Lucas grunted and rolled his eyes at the distinction. "Alright. But, that doesn't explain your friend."

Heaving out a beleaguered sigh, May crossed her arms tightly over her chest. "Piffles has always been trouble!" she grumbled. "But, since he crashed that beastly car of his into the river, he's been absolutely insufferable!"

Luc quirked an eyebrow at the girl's assertion. "Insufferable doesn't exactly cover trying to murder me in my sleep. And, what the hell did you do to me earlier? I felt like an intruder in my own body!"

"That wasn't me!"

"Sure looked like you," Lucas contended, rubbing at sleep crusted eyes.

"Piffles has tapped into the dark side of the spirit realm. He can take on other forms. And, he's mastered the art of possession," May confessed. "Oh, and I'm sorry about that," she said with a nod at Lucas as he rubbed at the scar on his back. "The only thing that breaks Piffles loose is pain."

The flush on the girl's cheeks made Lucas suspicious. "What did you do to me?" he tensely rumbled. An inaudible reply was his answer. "May?!" he pressed.

"I hit you with a shovel," she whispered to her shoes. "But it was for your own good!"

Luc flopped backward onto the narrow bed and snorted in displeasure. How in god's name was he supposed to host songwriting retreats in a haunted motel?

* * * * *

"Come on and be my good luck charm," Elvis coaxed from the dark jukebox.

Lucas froze in wary expectation when the music started. Stilling his exertions against the hulking body of the Plymouth Barracuda, he waited – heart pounding, blood thrumming. Which presence was lurking nearby?

"I wouldn't do that if I were you," May admonished as she materialized behind the steering wheel of the old car.

Grunting, Luc redoubled his efforts to move the last piece of corroded junk from the garage. The salvage man would be more than happy to haul the rusted relic away for scrap. And, once it was gone, Lucas could concentrate on getting his building permits pushed through the city council.

"Listen to me!" the bossy female shrilled. "You can't get rid of this car!"

After multiple conversations with the gregarious ghost during the last several days, Lucas was convinced that eliminating the vehicle also meant dislocating the vengeful spirit attached to it. "How long do you think taunting that ghoul is going to work? You said this old car is Piffles' anchor to The Belmont. If it goes, so does he!" Lucas declared.

"No!" May wailed as she flew toward the unsuspecting man. With an odd squelching sound, she invaded sinew and bone for the first time – her flight through the physical mass suspended by sheer dint of will. Peering out through her host's blue eyes, May gloated. "Ha!"

Relegated to the back seat in his own body for the second time in as many days, Lucas gave a fierce growl. "Get out, May!"

Testing her control of Luc's deep voice, she piped up: "No!"

If there was such thing as a masculine giggle, then that was surely what emanated from Lucas' mouth as May practiced her command of his physique. With childish glee, May struck a bodybuilder's pose.

Then inspiration struck. "Oh!" she squealed in a deep baritone as she hurried through the service station to the freshly scrubbed restroom. Peering into the mirror above the sink, May delighted in making various expressions with Luc's face. "Hey, sweet thing," she commented in a sultry tone as she role-played.

"What are you doing?" Luc hissed from inside his shell.

May's sweet titter reverberated through Lucas' body, and she continued with her game. In the highest falsetto Luc's vocal cords could manage, May squeaked, "My! Aren't you handsome!"

"OUT. NOW!" Lucas roared from the odd prison.

Sobering, May gazed at the man reflected in the mirror. "Can't you feel him?" she questioned through internal dialogue. "Can't you feel that pressure . . . the force against the top of your skull?"

Lucas worriedly acknowledged the odd sensation – something he imagined a deep-sea diver might experience as they descended into the murky depths.

"If I go, Piffles will take my place." May's thoughts played in the theatre of Luc's mind, and the images she transmitted were horrifying – scenes of Piffles' previous mayhem and destruction while in possession of a physical host. "Well?" she nervously questioned of her captive.

* * * * *

"Out, May!" Lucas roared, surprised to feel his flesh pull like taffy.

"Um, we might have a problem," May stammered several minutes later. "I've never done this before, and I'm not quite sure how to shake you loose," she bashfully admitted before an idea blossomed. Rushing toward the rickety workbench at the back of the shop, she hefted an old hammer. "Hold on! I have an idea."

"Don't you dare!" Lucas bellowed in alarm when the outrageous wraith laid his hand out on the workbench. "That's my picking hand!"

Amiably, May repositioned the implement and let the hammer slip free over Lucas' left foot.

With a yowl of pain, Lucas resumed control and scorched the air with every bit of profanity he could recall. "What in the holy hell?!" he gasped as he hopped around.

"That hurt!" May whimpered as she floated to rest atop the workbench.

Grunting, Luc resisted making a sarcastic remark as he gingerly put pressure on his damaged foot. "I think I'll take my chances with Piffles." he snapped.

"Don't say that!" May admonished. "He won't bother you while you are injured, but once that is feeling better," she tapered off before gesturing to the damage. "Well, I don't think I can watch!"

Galled, Luc griped, "You really get under my skin!"

An impish grin broke through the pout on May's face, and she giggled hysterically. "I do, don't I?" she teased. "But that is better than Piffles tormenting you, right?"

The considering survey May made of him from top to toes made Lucas pause. "Whatever you're thinking . . . just stop!" he protested, wary of the sly glint in the young woman's eyes.

"Actually, it is a very good idea," she asserted. "Your mortal pain is amplified in the spirit realm. It is what makes hell such a fearsome place – all the anguish of a lifetime magnified ten-thousand fold," May explained. "But, that works in your favor. As long as you are in agony, Piffles won't bother you!"

Sarcastically, Lucas muttered, "Great plan. I'll just have you whack me in the back of the head every couple of days."

"Alright," May nodded agreeably.

"Kidding, you twit!" Luc huffed. "I've got to get this car out of here! If it is gone, so is Primrose Piffles."

Disconsolately, May shook her head. "It doesn't work that way. Piffles is anchored by the car, but he's consigned to this place of broken dreams just like I am. If you take away his anchor, then he is free to roam!"

"And that is a bad thing?" Lucas peevishly concluded as he watched his own dreams circle the drain.

With a vigorous nod, May solemnly affirmed, "A very bad thing indeed."

"Trouble"

Lucas Barnes turned in startled anticipation when a high-pitched buzzing, like a swarm of angry bees, coalesced into the familiar dulcet tones of Presley. "If you're looking for trouble; you've come to the right place," the King of Rock n' Roll pronounced to a heavy Blues accompaniment.

Scrunching his eyes closed, Luc took a deep breath and then stomped on his own foot. The pain-filled grimace that crossed his face said he'd found the tender spot left from May's well-placed hammer attack earlier in the week.

When Lucas dared to open his eyes, the frenzied middle-aged ghoul let out a maniacal laugh that raised every hair on Luc's body.

"Because I'm evvvvil . . . my middle name is misery," the specter roared in a fearsome wail along with the Elvis tune. As he sang, Primrose Piffles advanced against the meddlesome mortal, herding him toward the open doorway that led to the cellar underneath the café. "Oh, yes, I'm evil! So, don't you mess around with me!"

Flailing, Lucas realized too late what was happening. The deranged ghost bared his teeth in a feral smile and propelled Luc through the air with the force of his hatred.

Pin-wheeling his arms, Lucas tumbled down the old wooden staircase – top over tails – a resounding shout of surprise echoing in his ears.

A snarl of satisfaction left spittle dribbling down Piffles chin, and he slammed the heavy wooden door to the basement with malicious glee. Throwing home the slide bolt, he rattled the door for ominous effect. Insane laughter echoed through the ramshackle building as Piffles dissolved into a putrid mist, and then it was silent.

* * * * *

Officer Haley Mitchell waved at the fire crew and stared in disgust at the charred mess of smelly mattresses. She was overly familiar with the havoc caused by mischief makers when it came to the abandoned property. But she'd hoped with a new owner in residence at The Belmont the nuisance calls would come to an end.

"Mr. Barnes?" Haley called as she entered the run-down building. Soft sounds of a radio playing led her through the nearly empty space, and Haley marveled at how quickly the place had been cleared out. "Mr. Barnes?" she questioned again as she moved through the kitchen to the back of the restaurant.

"Down here," a ragged voice called.

Mystified by the direction of the sound, Officer Mitchell responded, "Where are you?"

"Down here," Lucas breathlessly forced out. "The base . . . ment."

Staggered by the implications of the locked door, Haley slipped the bolt free and cautiously considered her surroundings. Senses on high-alert, Haley called for back-up before descending into the dank, dark cellar. When her flashlight beam caught sight of the crumpled man at the bottom of the rickety staircase, the policewoman sucked in a breath of disbelief. Barring an injured man in the basement wasn't just adolescent shenanigans!

The metallic scent of blood hit Haley's nose as she bent to examine Luc's still form. The poor fellow struggled to breathe, and the sticky pool under Luc's head declared his urgent need for help. With an unsteady hand, Haley keyed the mic on her shoulder and called for an ambulance. A bare minute later, two members of the fire crew thundered down the steps with a medical kit. "I need to secure the scene," she quietly commented before she relinquished care of the victim.

* * * * *

Lucas tentatively traced the line of dainty stitches that followed the hinge of his jaw before it disappeared under his left ear and down the side of his neck. The jagged piece of wood that tore his face open on his descent into the darkness had scarcely missed his jugular vein. But it was the piercing ache in his chest that stole Luc's breath.

"I don't know," he mumbled again. The barrage of questions about his "accident" made Luc physically ill. Or, maybe it was the heavy narcotics swimming through his bloodstream. Either way, there was no way to answer Officer Mitchell's inquires without sounding deranged!

"You didn't see or hear anything before you were shoved down the basement stairs?" Haley pressed.

In the darkened room, Lucas fought the waves of pain that radiated through his chest and shoulder. "Could we do this another time?" he groaned.

Sensitive to the man's discomfort, Haley nodded. "Of course, Mr. Barnes. I'll come back when you're feeling better." As she turned to go, the policewoman added, "We'll be sending a regular patrol past your place until we catch this firebug. The Belmont has been a target for random fires through the years, but whoever did this . . ."

Squinting through swollen eyes, Lucas focused his attention on the officer. "Firebug?"

"Unless you were planning to torch the whole place . . ."

"No!" Lucas growled with as much force as he could muster. "How much damage?"

With a sigh, Haley moved closer to the angry man's bedside. "None of the buildings were involved, Mr. Barnes. Still, you've got quite a mess of burned up mattresses and other trash out there. It kind of looks like a whirlwind picked everything up and scattered it around while it was burning. There are scorch marks in a few places on the exterior of the café, but otherwise, it's just a matter of clean-up."

Under his breath, Luc furiously mumbled, "If you weren't already dead, Piffles, I'd kill you myself!"

Haley's eyebrows shot up when she caught the patient's quiet rant. "Care to explain, Mr. Barnes?"

* * * * *

Lucas Barnes' claims of supernatural activity at The Belmont rankled Haley to no end. Ghosts and ghouls were definitely out of her bailiwick! But, the ring of veracity in the man's statements, and a series of probing questions about long-gone individuals couldn't be ignored.

Disgruntled by her gullibility, Haley ran a critical eye over the hulking shadows of the low-slung buildings on the Barnes property before getting out of her Jeep. She jangled the hefty ring of keys Luc provided and huffed out a nervous breath. "Hallucinations brought on by pain medication," Haley mumbled reassuringly to herself as she stepped out into the cold night air. "That's it – a head injury and heavy narcotics," she quietly asserted as she approached the derelict buildings.

Kicking away debris from the earlier blaze, the testy woman marched up the lopsided steps of the café and jammed the appropriate key into the lock. "May! May Levy!" she shouted into the gloom as she entered the room. "Come out and talk to me." The nearly indistinct tones of a soft polka raised Haley's hackles.

"Please don't break my heart in two . . . that's not hard to do . . ."

Whirling toward the sound of the music, Haley expected to see the tabletop jukebox Luc mentioned. But the room was still wreathed in shadow.

"'Cause I don't have a wooden heart."

Haley squinted into the gloomy room and scrunched up her nose at the "oompah" beat. "Accordion music? Really?" she complained to the prankster. "I thought you had a penchant for Presley?"

"You shouldn't be here," a soft voice advised from near her left ear.

Ignoring the goosebumps that rippled up her arm, Haley pivoted and firmly questioned, "Do you have information about what happened here today?"

"You need to go. Piffles is in a BAD mood."

Peeved by the mention of a man who'd been worm fodder for over three decades, Haley commented, "I'd be grouchy too if I'd been stuck in this dump for thirty years."

"He thinks you're pretty," the girlish voice tittered.

"Oh, for Pete's sake," Haley thought. Just what she needed – a ghost on the make. "Who are you?" she demanded. "Show yourself!"

A subtle shift in the shadows morphed and transitioned into a soft luminance that grew brighter and more distinct as it moved. In the back corner of the restaurant, the light coalesced and began to take shape.

Under a spotlight of sorts, two people appeared out of the haze and sat down across from each other in the corner booth. The vinyl seats creaked in protest as fannies slid across their surface, and Haley watched in dumbfounded amazement as the scene came alive. Dishes clanked, the sound of other diners just out of sight peppered the air with an unintelligible conversation, and a waitress materialized at the table with two milkshakes. The sweet scent of chocolate and whipped cream hit Haley's nostrils and her mouth watered as the couple in the booth sampled their treat.

Haley's perception of distance distorted the girlish laughter of the teenager and the soft Southern drawl of the young man, but their flirtatious manner was obvious. Bright eyes and a flush on the girl's cheeks gave away her intense interest in the raven-haired fellow. With his back to the room, Haley couldn't watch the boy's expression, but his body language spoke volumes!

The spotlight that illuminated the tableau shifted and expanded until it revealed a full-size jukebox to the left of the corner booth, and the sultry sound of "I Want You, I Need You, I Love You" began to play softly.

Caught up in observing the tender romance as it played out, Haley wandered closer.

"You know I want to . . . but, I can't stay, May," the young man replied to the girl's teary pleas.

"You could drive tow truck for the service station," she protested, grabbing for her beau.

Slowly untangling their hands, the gentle fellow shook his head and slid from the booth. "I'm sorry. But, I gotta go," he soothed before turning.

Shocked to be caught eavesdropping, Haley retreated, and then gaped in open-mouthed disbelief as the very familiar man stepped right through her!

An Artic breeze stole Haley's breath and stiffened her form. With an unsteady gait, she approached the booth and awkwardly slid across the red vinyl seat. Facing the weeping girl, Haley's high-pitched voice wavered, "Was that . . .?"

"My Aaron," May whispered, clasping a fist to her heart. "He left me," she despondently cried. In response, the tune in the air made an ear-splitting, screeching halt.

Abruptly the driving voice of the King wailed, "It's down at the end of Lonely Street . . . at Heartbreak Hotel."

And with that, May vanished.

With a solid "thunk!" Haley's backside hit the bare floor, and she looked around in stupefied amazement. Scrambling to her feet, the practical, no-nonsense officer frantically searched the darkness for the booth, the jukebox, anything!

Nothing.

Zilch.

Nada.

All that was left was the same empty room Haley had searched earlier in the day.

* * * * *

"Primrose Percival Piffles," Haley explained with a look at her notes.

"Jeez! Did his parents hate the kid?" Lucas commented with a bleak look at the disheveled woman.

"I don't know. Not many people remember the guy," Haley replied with another glance at some old newspaper clippings. Sliding a photocopy of the article across the bedside tray, she continued. "His parents were hog farmers south of town. By the time he was in high school, he already had a rap sheet. Mild stuff by our standards, but hot rodding and a few run-ins with the local sheriff in the 50s earned him a reputation."

Luc skimmed the newspaper story, and his eyebrows went up. "According to this, Piffles deliberately ran that old Barracuda into the lake."

"Yeah. Just outside of town," Haley confirmed. "Rammed the other driver he was racing and sent them both to a watery grave."

His busted ribs screamed when Lucas tried to shift into a more comfortable position. "So, what am I going to do with a weepy wraith and a sinister, spiteful spirit?"

"Hey, I only handle law and order on the flesh and blood side of things. You want help with ghouls and goblins, I suggest you call the "Ghost Hunters," Haley chided. "But, I wouldn't plan on going back to The Belmont until you figure it out."

With a crabby grunt, Lucas scowled at his unusual ally. "Where exactly am I supposed to go? I have a contractor starting work on the motel units next week, and they still aren't cleaned out!"

"Suppose you can get May to straighten things up?" Haley teased with a wink.

Luc slatted a perturbed look at the sassy woman and grumbled, "She's not my fairy godmother. And, I don't think she can 'bibbity-boppity-boo' that crap into the dumpster."

"You never know unless you ask."

Rolling his eyes in exasperation, Luc made a small gesture toward the female officer. "Since Piffles has taken a shine to you, why don't you run on over and make that suggestion. And, while you're at it, tell that demonic fiend he better get used to company. I've got five songwriters from Chicago signed up for the spring retreat. And, *I'LL* burn the place to the ground before I let Primrose Percival Piffles screw this up!"

* * * * *

"He seems like a perfectly nice, um . . . spirit," Haley reaffirmed. "Piffles just doesn't like being teased all the time."

Lucas turned a disgruntled glance toward the wholly sincere woman and glared. "Have you lost your mind?" he hotly questioned with a gesture toward his face and then his busted-up torso. "Four broken ribs, a dislocated shoulder, and enough stitches to make a child's garment!"

Haley had the good grace to blush and concede, "Okay. Maybe he got a little carried away. But you tried getting rid of his car. I really think he's just . . . well, I don't know. Misunderstood?"

"Officer Haley Mitchell, counselor to the damned," Luc muttered disagreeably under his breath.

Aiming a glowering "stink eye" at the irritable man, Haley retorted, "I heard that!"

"Good! Then hear this . . . I'M NOT FIXING PIFFLES' STUPID CAR!" The rest of the short trip home passed in stilted silence, but Lucas' was adamant. He was not spending a single penny on restoring some hobgoblin's ride!

The crunch of gravel served to remind Luc of the mess that waited for him, and he looked up – expecting a disaster zone. Instead, he found several people moving around the property with shovels and garbage bags, including his electrician. "Hey! What's going on?"

"These folks have family ties to The Belmont," Haley tightly explained. "And, they want to see it opened back up."

Cousins, grandchildren, nieces, and nephews. It was a hodge-podge family reunion in his parking lot! Utterly perplexed by their willing assistance, Luc cautiously accepted the group's well wishes and listened to the details of their clean up efforts. But the kid that caught his eye carried an eerie resemblance to his ghoulish nemesis. "You a Piffle?" he gruffly asked.

Going scarlet, the teenager went wide-eyed and slowly nodded. "My grandmom," he explained. "She was related to the guy who worked in the garage here."

"You gonna give me trouble too?" Lucas groused as he cradled his sore ribs. A hush fell over the helpers, and it was Luc's turn to flush in embarrassment. "Sorry, kid," he mumbled apologetically. "I'm having a hell of a day. Shouldn't have taken it out on you."

Intervening, Haley steered the ornery man toward one of the motel units. "You're supposed to be taking it easy," she diplomatically observed with a conspiratorial wink at the others. "And, I think it's time for more of your pain killers."

"Where are we going?" Luc protested when they were out of earshot of the clean-up crew. "My camper's parked in the garage!"

Ignoring Lucas' grumbled admonishment, the persistent woman shuffled him along and pointed to Unit 1. "We, ah, had a bit of a problem in one of the service bays yesterday." Once they were safely ensconced in the ragtag room, Haley closed the door and sheepishly admitted, "Piffles . . . well, he, um . . . he flattened your camper when he found out I was bringing you back here."

Dead air hung between them as Lucas processed the announcement.

Abashed, the suddenly timid lady mumbled, "I, ah, had the crew get rid of the rubble. So, you don't need to worry about that!" Waving to a cardboard box sitting in the corner, Haley advised, "We saved what we could."

Lucas stared at the small container in bewilderment. "What you could?" he parroted. "What you could?!" he bellowed when the reality hit him square between the eyes. "Where is my stuff? WHERE IS MY GUITAR!?"

With her back propped against the exterior door, Haley went stiff when the furious man spun in her direction. Steel in her spine and authority in her voice, she lowly stated, "Stand down, Lucas."

Roaring like a wounded grizzly, Luc stomped around the small confines of the motel room – enraged by the limitations of his injured body and the ominous, unsettled dread in his gut. An unmistakable certainty, a fearful anticipation . . . it covered Lucas in a cold sweat. His whole world was crashing down. And there wasn't a damn thing he could do to stop it!

The Belmont

Comeupance

Unsettled by the recent mayhem at The Belmont, May Levy restlessly paced between the front door and the bathroom. Her protective instincts were on high alert when it came to the dark-haired man sprawled out across the narrow bed. Luc's injuries were mild by Piffles' standards; but the melancholy mortal had no way of knowing that. "Leave him alone, Prim," May shouted into the spirit realm. "He means you no harm."

A maniacal laugh chased gooseflesh up May's arms – an odd situation considering her lack of a material body. But there was no denying the sinister spirit's violent and often horrific manipulation of those who wandered into his realm. And, May's gentle nature abhorred the beastly ghoul's sense of justice – penalties that Primrose Piffles considered reasonable compensation for the indignities he endured during his lifetime.

"He is not Aaron," May pointed out. "You have no reason to hate Lucas."

The smell of rotten eggs blossomed and fanned out as the fearsome poltergeist made his appearance at the edge of the small hotel room. But, for this one moment, Piffles chose to appear in his youthful state – much as May preferred to do. "You fawn over him, May," the specter waspishly snapped. "Besides, it is fun to torment him," Piffles snickered as his form began to crackle and spark around the edges.

Wringing her hands, May pleaded, "Please, don't hurt him." Approaching the ominous presence, she softened her voice. "For the sake of whatever good feelings you held for me, Prim. Please, won't you let Lucas be?"

Snarling, Piffles shouted, "You destroyed whatever I felt for you when you took up with that singer!" And, with that, he burst into blue flames and a puff of putrid smoke.

* * * * *

Lucas woke to the sound of whimpering. But when he cautiously tried to move his aching body, he felt oddly disjointed. Cracking one swollen eye open, Luc irritably groused, "Not again!"

"Good morning," May timidly blubbered. Her host's injuries seared May's heightened perceptions of anguish; but, she refused to abandon the man to Piffles' demented plans.

"What are you doing, May?" Lucas huffed in exasperation from inside his bodily shell. This whole "possession" bit was getting mighty old, mighty fast.

Leery of causing her host any additional discomfort, May gingerly moved the man's large body into an upright position before she stopped to gasp. Luc's mortal pain was amplified to extraordinary proportions in May's realm of existence; and, the torment was unbearable!

"May?!" Lucas anxiously prompted, highly disturbed by the wraith's distressed moans.

"Take two aspirin and call me in the morning," he softly teased, advising the suffering spirit of the relief offered in his pill bottle. "WHOA!!" he scolded when four of the narcotics made an appearance behind his lips. "I said, 'two!' Are you trying to knock me out?!" Lucas exclaimed from inside his fleshy prison.

Clasping the man's muscular arms around his midsection, May groaned and anxiously waited to see if the pain medicine would make a difference to her perception of Lucas' bodily harm. With gradual effect, the searing intensity of her human host's misery eased; and, May sighed in profound relief.

"Out, May!" Luc demanded, kicking at the back of his knee caps.

"Don't . . . do . . . that," May whined. After a few more minutes, she eased off the bed and stumbled toward the dismal bathroom. Peeling metallic gold wallpaper with bright pink embossed flowers blinded her as soon as the light went on; and, May lifted one of Luc's bulky arms to block the glare.

In the cracked mirror over the sink, she stared into the reflection of Lucas' blue gaze. "There is no other way to keep you safe . . . unless you plan to leave The Belmont today," she chided, the sleepy baritone booming around the tiny space.

Lucas growled out a fierce string of profanity before questioning: "But, can't Piffles dislodge you the same way you chased him off the other night?"

Abashed, May mumbled to the reflection: "I have no idea. I've never done this before, but I'll get rid of the shovel if that makes you feel better."

"I'd feel better if I could take a leak," Luc absently groused before a flash of insight made him stutter to a stop. "Don't you dare!"

But May couldn't help herself. She giggled and looked down at the drawstring of the cotton sleep pants.

"May!" Lucas vehemently protested when the impish spirit tugged the waistband open. "Hands off!"

"They are your hands," May reminded, her girlish titter sounding like the buzz of a snare drum roll in Luc's deep voice. "And, it's not like I haven't seen one of these before," she calmly informed the mortified man.

"I don't need to know that, May Levy!" Luc abruptly chided. "Now get your hands, er . . . get my hands . . . oh, Jesus!" he stammered. "Just leave well enough alone!"

"Aaron never minded when I touched . . ."

"STOP! Just stop!" Lucas huffed out, his thoughts mutinous.

The man's rioting ideas brought a halt to May's mischief, and she worriedly questioned, "Who's Richie? I won't be a part of causing someone harm!"

"I'm gonna strangle him!" Lucas bellowed from behind his sternum. "Opportunity of a lifetime, my ass!" he yelled before stuttering to a halt. "Levy? Oh, shit! You're related to Richie, aren't you? You're that crazy aunt with the tall tales!" Lucas groaned.

Taken aback, May demanded, "Explain yourself," as she wiggled uncomfortably. Her host really needed a bigger bladder if he was going to be shy about this whole "possession" thing.

"Rich Levy . . . my cousin . . . he sold me this place. Had the nerve to call it the 'opportunity of a lifetime,'" Lucas stridently answered. "And, the next time I see him, I'm going to whack him over the head with the shovel!"

"Aunt! That's what you said," May reminded. "You called me this boy's aunt."

Lucas grunted disagreeably. He might not be in control of his bodily functions, but he could certainly still feel the impulses – and his back teeth were swimming. Heaving out a long-suffering sigh, Luc snapped, "If you are the lady who played the piano in the café, then you are Richie's aunt."

The wail that burst forth shocked Luc, and he shrunk back in embarrassment when his jailer dissolved into tears. "Ah, could you not do that," he inquired, peeved to be included in the ghostly hysterics. Peeking out through the storm, Lucas could only imagine what he looked like to the rest of the world – a beat-up, muscle-bound man hunched down on a small toilet, crying his eyes out. Argh!

"Um, there, there," he awkwardly cajoled, patting the reverse side of his clavicle in an attempt at comfort. "Aw, jeez . . . I won't clobber him. Okay?"

* * * * *

Rich Levy dropped his cigarette into the gravel and crushed it with the heel of his highly polished boot. His cousin's out-of-the-blue "distress call" irritated him to no end. "Come on, Dad," Richie said as he leaned back into his freshly-detailed, meticulously restored '67 Mustang. "This is the place."

After prying himself from the confines of the sports car, A.J. Levy glanced around at the ragtag group of buildings and grinned. "You wouldn't believe half the stories I heard about this place," he jovially commented. "Supposedly, it was where all the up and coming 'hep cats' of the day came to play their music."

"I know. You told me." *Ad nauseum* Richie thought begrudgingly. After hours alone in the car with his father and the ribald re-hashing of ancient history, Rich was more than ready for this "errand of mercy" to be over.

* * * * *

"Knock it off!" Lucas hissed from inside his shell as May went weepy. "Jesus, May! Men don't cry all over each other," he vehemently protested.

But there was no help for it. And, when his mother's younger half brother gently patted him on the shoulder? Yeah. Lucas knew he'd never live the moment down.

Thankfully his tender ribs and shoulder limited some of May's control over his body; or, he'd likely have both his uncle and cousin in a bear hug!

Uncomfortable with his crazy cousins' antics and his father's nostalgic whimsy, Richie prompted, "Get your stuff; and, let's go, Luc."

All a flutter, May joyfully clasped at the older man's hand – and ignored her host's rapid-fire barrage of protest at her behavior. In Luc's deep voice, she extolled, "I have so much to tell you!"

* * * * *

At the end of a long shift, all Officer Haley Mitchell wanted to do was head home for some "R&R" before the Trick or Treaters arrived. Yet, she found her Jeep headed down Old Route 66 in the direction of The Belmont as soon as she was free from her patrol duties. "Hey! Should you be out of bed?" she demanded when Haley spotted Lucas coming out of the old café.

The radiant smile that stretched Luc's black and blue face surprised the policewoman; but, her mouth dropped open in disbelief at the masculine giggle and demure wave of welcome. Haley snapped her jaw shut and then blinked in amazement when she discovered that Lucas was holding hands with an older man. "So that's the way the wind blows," she mumbled under her breath.

"Come meet my A.J.!" May called to the woman. Wholly engrossed in the joyful reunion, May was utterly forgetful of the man she represented to the world. At least until the spiteful fellow started banging at the back of a very sore rib cage.

"May!! So help me . . ." Luc shouted, unhinged by the whole kooky situation.

Ignoring the angry internal voice, May tugged A.J. forward and led the little parade of people to the larger of the two houses on the property. "Here, let me show you," she enthused in the very masculine tones of her host.

Aggravated by the delay in their departure, Rich disagreeably howled, "We need to get on the road, Lucas. I don't want to spend the night in this one-horse town!"

Exasperated by the rude behavior, May tapped one finger against Richie's mouth and admonished, "Behave, young man!"

At the reprimand, Richie's face scrunched up in horrified indignation. In response, Lucas couldn't help but chuckle at his cousin's chagrined displeasure. As a weary battle victim of a supernatural war for dominance, Lucas was in a riotous state of dishevel; so, he took great joy in seeing the prideful, money-grubbing pain in the ass get his comeuppance.

* * * * *

The interior of the old home was musty and dusty; but, it was a treasure trove of memorabilia. And, as the afternoon had turned to early evening, Haley was stunned to realize that the two new visitors also had a family connection to The Belmont.

"Well, my hands are shakin', and my knees are weak," Elvis crooned from out of nowhere.

Startled by the sudden serenade, Haley jumped and then laughed as the song continued.

"What's so funny?" Luc mumbled as he tried in vain to dislodge the gregarious ghost from his person. The odd "show and tell" May insisted upon was making Lucas batty.

Unaware of Luc's "possession" predicament, Haley chuckled. "Are you feeling 'All Shook Up,' Mr. Barnes?" she teased, intrigued by the sudden onset of his very feminine mannerisms.

Arms tightly crossed over his chest, Richie scowled in sullen annoyance. The endless chatter about long-gone musicians and the display of faded photographs bored him to tears. But, his father avidly soaked up every last little bit of the eccentric review.

"Don't really remember my Aunt May," A.J. commented as he stared at the old photo he'd been offered. "She died young, I think. My folks didn't talk about her much . . . except to laugh over her tall tales."

A bubble of displeasure rose behind Luc's sternum; and, he recoiled as May's temper boiled through his veins. And, it was his voice that snapped, "Of course they laughed. They never believed a word I said about my Aaron! Oh, they stole away with his child and called me an unfit mother; but, they never considered . . ."

May's ire turned to shame as everyone in the room turned their avid attention on Lucas. And, she shuddered inside the body she held captive.

Internally, Lucas carefully prompted, "What are you saying, May?"

Silenced stretched like a hangman's noose. Then, his fists pounded against his chest; and, a fireball blossomed behind Luc's breastbone. He howled in agony; and, Lucas clutched his damaged ribcage as he reclaimed control of his injured body. Gasping for breath, Luc hoarsely uttered every vile imprecation he could recall. "Damn you, May," he finally ground out.

The high keening of the anguished soul's wail became audible to the other's as the incorporeal being flitted about the room. Frantically, May rummaged for the photograph that would vindicate her; and, when she found it, the young woman shouted in triumph.

With a shooing motion, the determined ghost gestured Lucas aside and perched next to the petrified gentleman she claimed as her own. "Your father," she softly announced to A.J. before handing over the black and white picture.

Stupified, A.J. Levy shook his head to clear his vision. But, the vision held! And, the very distinct form of the young woman he knew to be his deceased Aunt May was sitting next to him!

A.J.'s blue gaze caught with hers. "My father was Richard Levy," he stuttered in confusion before he looked down. His breath caught. He knew the man in the photo! *Nearly everyone in the world knew the man in the photo!* A.J. thought in stunned disbelief.

Running an unsteady hand through the thinning hair that had once been just as black as his purported father's, A.J.'s glance bounced around the room. And, when his gaze locked with that of his startled son, the truth hit home. Those same eyes were staring back at him from the sixty-five-year-old photograph in his hand. "How?" A.J. managed to say.

"My brother, Richard . . . the man you knew as your father . . . he took you from me when you were eight months old. And, he had me institutionalized for over a year," May quietly announced. "I was an unwed mother. My brother never believed me . . . never considered that my Aaron . . ."

From his place near the open window, Richie emerged from his bewildered haze and began to rant, "I'm Richard Levy. I am named for my grandfather!" Shooting to his feet, the angry man bellowed, "I am not related to some crazy woman who cut her wrists because some overweight singer overdosed!"

Tugging at the sleeves of her pink mohair sweater, May shrunk away from her irate grandson. The scars on her wrists marked her as one of the damned – an irrefutable, undeniable impression that consigned her to endlessly wander the scene of her broken dreams.

Agitated in the extreme, Rich flipped his cigarette toward the window with shaking fingers - only to realize his mistake as soon as the hot butt landed near a pile of crumbling boxes. With a whoosh, the dry paper ignited; and, a sudden breeze swirled the fiery scraps around in a whirlwind conflagration. In an instant, the packed room was alight with new flames, as years worth of old files and photographs were consumed.

May shrieked as the tattered curtains fell over Richie's head in a waterfall of racing flames. "Richard!" she wailed as the pompous man tried to beat down the searing blaze that set his clothing alight.

Lucas choked as the bitter smoke filled his lungs. Awkwardly, he painfully lurched to his feet and then fell back as another draft toppled a precarious tower of crates. The terrified screams of his family members and the scent of burnt flesh pummeled his senses; but, Lucas could not move!

Frantic to free Lucas, Haley began to remove the debris that pinned him while A.J. tried to smother the flames that engulfed Richie.

Screeching wildly, May's ethereal form rippled like waves on a pond when A.J. collapsed over his son's charred form. "Aaron! Aaron Junior!" May chanted in a wretched wail as she clung to her long-lost child.

Overwhelmed by the intensity of the flames and the dense smoke, Haley toppled to the floor near Lucas – her chest heaving to process the superheated air. As a last consolation, the fallen officer clasped Luc's hand before she closed her eyes against the sting of floating embers.

"Haley!" Lucas rasped as he gave a convulsive shudder. Then he heaved with all his might and dislodged the rest of the towering inferno that had him pinned.

Moments later, the squall of sirens pierced the air as Lucas Barnes stumbled from the flames with the unconscious body of Officer Haley Mitchell. His seared flesh and broken body screamed in agony as he gasped for air; but, the subtle rise and fall of Haley's chest said there was still a chance for her survival.

* * * * *

Patting the edge of the hospital bed, Haley gestured the weary man forward. "Thank you, Lucas," she hoarsely whispered. Her mind had spent hours turning over those last few seconds before she lost consciousness. "How did you get us out?" Haley finally asked.

"There was no one else left," he tensely answered before he took her hand.

"I am sorry, Luc," Haley gasped, staggered by the senseless loss.

Lowering his voice, Lucas quietly disclosed, "May is gone as well."

"She's free? Her spirit is free?" the injured woman questioned.

"Her family is together now, just like May wanted," he ground out.

A comfortable silence settled between them; and, Haley stroked the back of Luc's hand. "What will you do now?" she eventually inquired. "Will you stay in Litchfield?"

Blue eyes sparked impishly and sparkled as he nodded. "The Belmont will open in the spring. Just like planned."

Urging Lucas closer, Haley whispered, "What about Piffles?"

"Don't worry. I've taken care of him," the musician said with an overwide grin.

Released from the shackles of the unrequited love he'd held for his only childhood friend, Primrose Piffles made the final transition into the demonic realm. And with that power in his grasp, there was nothing left to detour him from wreaking vengeance.

From inside his fleshy prison, Lucas Barnes recoiled as the malevolent ghoul's fiendish plans played through the theatre of his mind. "No!" he bellowed into the echoing cavern of his chest cavity as his mortal form leaned in to place a sensual kiss on Haley's cherry lips.

YOU CAN MAKE A BIG DIFFERENCE!

If you enjoyed this story
please consider leaving
an honest review -
it is the best way to thank an author.

Customer Reviews are the most powerful tool we have as Independent Authors for increasing interest our books. The cost of advertising, like the big publishing houses, is cost prohibitive; but, we have something more powerful and effective . . . **YOU!**

A COMMITTED AND LOYAL BUNCH OF READERS leaving honest reviews of our books help other people discover our stories. So, if you have enjoyed this book, we would be very grateful if you would spend a couple of minutes leaving a review on Amazon, Goodreads, or Bookbub about what you liked and didn't like - it can be as short as you want.

Thank you so much!

Rick Barr
rick@barr26.com

Michele Dalton
author@michelepollockdalton.com

Rick Barr

Musician, Audio Narrator, and Voice Professional, Rick Barr is the voice for numerous audiobooks. But, his first love is that good ole' time rock n' roll. Based out of Columbus, Ohio, he can be found at numerous entertainment venues sharing his talent.

Listen to the live narration of each episode of "The Belmont:"

Episode 1: https://tinyurl.com/yyl5w7lu

Episode 2: https://tinyurl.com/yxao8r79

Episode 3: https://tinyurl.com/yxgxrmpr

Follow me:

 www.RicksVoice.com

 www.Facebook.com/RickBarrVoiceovers

 www.twitter.com/RicksVoice26

Michele Pollock Dalton

My name is Michele Pollock Dalton; and, I am an unapologetic romantic. While most romance writers focus specifically on falling in love, I have chosen to write about people staying in love - living each day in a way that celebrates their relationship and focuses on building a strong, unbreakable bond.

Most days are spent wheeling around after a remarkable little boy that I love with all my heart. And, sometimes I put my domestic goddess skills to work, so we don't have to run around naked =)

White chocolate truffles and faith fuel my writing endeavors; and, my sincere hope is that the characters I invent resonate with folks who need a bit of inspiration to face their day.

Stop in for a visit at:

www.MichelePollockDalton.com

for extra tidbits, character vignettes, and free downloads.

I look forward to meeting you there.

Follow me:

 www.MichelePollockDalton.com

 www.Facebook.com/OfficialMichelePollockDalton

 www.Pinterest.com/MichelePollockDalton

Copyrights

Episode 1:

"Are You Lonesome Tonight." Written by Lou Handman and Roy Turk. Made popular by Elvis Presley / 1960

Episode 2:

"Honky Tonk Side of Town." Written by Michele Pollock Dalton / 1994

"Devil in Disguise." Written by Bill Giant, Bernie Baum, and Florence Kaye. Made popular by Elvis Presley / 1963

"Good Luck Charm." Written by Aaron Schroder and Wally Gold. Published by Gladys Music. Made popular by Elvis Presley / 1961

Episode 3:

"Trouble." Written by Jerry Lieber and Mike Stoller. Made popular by Elvis Presley / 1958

"Wooden Heart." Written by Fred Wise, Ben Weisman, Kay Twomey, and Bert Kaempfert. Made popular by Elvis Presley / 1964

"Heartbreak Hotel." Written by Tommy Burden, Mae Boren, and Elvis Presley. Made popular by Elvis Presley / 1956

Episode 4:

"All Shook Up." Written by Otis Blackwell and Elvis Presley. Published by Elvis Presley. Made popular by Elvis Presley / 1957

www.ingramcontent.com/pod-product-compliance
Lightning Source LLC
Chambersburg PA
CBHW020606130626
46552CB00007B/3075